HANDYMAN SEX COLLECTION

EXPLICIT DIRTY EROTICA SHORT STORIES

MELISA POCHE

plicit Press

CHAPTER 1

CUM RESET MY BUTTONS: HANDY MAN 1

DAMN IT! My internet is out again! I am so tired of resetting my router and modem. That's it I'm calling the cable guy. He better fix it correctly this time or else. I got on the phone and told the internet company I needed a cable guy out to my house pronto. I am a webcam model and my private shows can't wait. While waiting on my guy to arrive, I went ahead and got fixed up for my private show later. I put on my new little Bo Peep lingerie set I had ordered for a ridiculously low price online. The final touch was my pair of 6-inch silver stilettos. Damn, I looked hot as fuck, even if I did say so myself!

Just when I was about to get pissed off and call the cable company again, I hear a ring at the door. *It must be him*, I thought to myself. Well, he was just going to have to see me in my get-up. I didn't give a fuck what he thought! I clomped to the door in my silver heels and swung the door open with a touch of anger included in the swing. "Well, it's about damn time," I said sarcastically. "What took you so long?" "I don't know Miss Bo Peep. I guess I got held up by Little Red Riding Hood," said the cable guy very cynically.

"Very funny. The box is this way. Do you think you can fix it lickety-split? I have a show in an hour," I asked him very impatiently.

"I'll do my best ma'am. Don't have a fit." He said looking sheepishly as he headed for the box. I noticed as he bent over he sure had a fine ass on him. As a matter of fact, this dude was hot as fuck. He was getting me wet and warm in all the right places. In a way, this was a good thing and in another, I didn't want pussy juice stains on my little white thong. What the fuck! I needed to warm up so I laid back on my chaise lounge and started fingering my cunt like nobody's business. I really didn't care if cable boy heard the slippery sounds from the box where he was fiddling with wires. I had some fiddling of my own to do. It always helped to have a raging snatch before I went live.

The more I fingered the closer to an orgasm I was getting. If I got too close, I'd stop fingering for a minute or two and give my throbbing g-spot a rest. I could feel it bulging within the grips of my fingertips. I was getting extremely horny by now so I brought out my toy and squatted on it so my cunt could feel amazing fucking pressure within. I could also feel the thong string between my lips adding even more hot pressure as it pressed on my hard clit, causing me to gasp in ecstasy. I started to bounce lightly up and down on my drenched toy. I was getting so fucking wet I smeared some cunt cream on my left titty and started to suck and nibble.

I was really getting into my finger fucking session and had forgotten about cable guy temporarily, but I looked up just in time to see him looking at me play the fuck out of my cunt through the door crack. It appeared he liked what he saw by the size of the bulge in his blue slacks. I could see his stiff cock lying up by his belly and it was massive; at least 8 inches long.

On all fours, I leaned over the edge of my bed and motioned for him to come inside my bedroom. Without any words spoken, he entered inside my room and fervently attacked me with hot wet kisses. He ripped my thong off and started to eat my pussy like nobody's business. I lifted my ass up completely off of my bed and pushed his head down farther into my needy cunt. I was so horny I could hardly contain my greedy girl parts. He moved his head sideways and back and forth on my cunt so fast I could hardly see it. He sucked my clit and lapped on my lips like a starving animal. He was hungry to eat some pussy, it was easy to see that.

After making a feast out of my bald cunt, I begged the cable guy to fuck me hard before my show so that my pussy would be red and swollen. He slowly but assuredly slipped his long stiff meat inside my greedy snatch. Inch by excruciating inch he slid inside me. It felt very nice feeling his cock fill me up completely with rock-hard girth.

He sped up his intensity and started screwing me hard against the bedpost. I threw my legs up by his ears and took the banging like a good girl. The harder he banged the louder I screamed. I hadn't been fucked this hard in a long time. I grabbed his face, looked straight into his eyes and said, "Fuck me hard and fuck me now!" He did exactly as I asked and increased his intensity even more.

I bucked my body upwards towards his angry cock inside of me. I banged him as hard as he fucked me. We started to kiss. I yanked his head down towards me and we kissed and bit each other's tongues with ferocious force. I had never been screwed so wildly in my life and I fucking loved it! After exploding deep inside my raging snatch and my pussy grabbing his shaft and squirting, he simply got up, put on his pants, and walked out without saying a word.

I freshened up a bit and wiped the cum that was dribbling down my leg off with a cloth and turned on my internet and computer that was now working perfectly. It was definitely well worth the call to the cable man today, yes indeed.

CHAPTER 2

THE SPARKS FLY

WHEN A GIRL CAN'T EVEN RUN her washing machine and coffee pot at the same time, it's time to call an electrician. I am so tired of my breaker box tripping. It is a real pain in the ass. I have to climb a flight of stairs and go and flip the switch almost every day. That's it, I'm calling a man to come out and fix this. My lazy ass husband sure won't do it. He won't fix a damn thing around here.

He might get mad that we have a huge repair bill but I don't give a fuck. Sometimes a girl needs a hot cup of coffee while she watches her favorite soap opera you know what I mean?

I got my cell phone and dialed the first number I saw in the list of able electricians. As I sat on hold, I thumbed through my recent Playgirl edition. Damn it why can't I have a hunk mowing my lawn in only his tennis shoes? All I get is a beer-drinking slob on my couch every night.

. . .

That's my tough luck in life and it sucks, truly, it does. I finished making the call and was told to expect an electrician to my house by noontime. Great! Maybe he'd be done by the time my soap starts.

I went about a few chores and lost track of time until I heard the doorbell ring. Oh no! I was still running around braless in a tank top and my super short cut-offs. Oh well, I'm sure this guy has seen half-clothed women before in his profession. I went to the door and opened it up and my chin nearly hit the doorway step. He was fucking gorgeous! Usually, handymen were kind of yucky but not this guy. He was like something in a Hollywood movie. He was tall, built like a Greek god and he had boyish good looks that drove me wild. When he flashed a smile, I damn near melted on the spot. "I'm here to check your box ma'am," he said and I giggled. "Your breaker box I mean," as he cleared his throat.

"Come on in and I'll show you my box." I giggled again at the thought of it. I could swear I heard him moan under his breath. I turned around and he had his eyes on my swaying ass in front of him. Sure, he tried to look up quickly but I caught him staring. I did have a hot ass even if I did say so myself. I kind of gave him a cute smile and then showed him where the breaker box was.

It wasn't long until the hunk came into the living room where I was and said he thought he had my box working properly. I couldn't help it but I once again giggled and then for some reason I will never understand, I attacked the eager guy by the size of the boner in his jeans. Yes! I attacked him. I stood up, kissed him, and grabbed his cock through his work jeans. Much to my surprise, his cock was hard as fucking steel.

I don't usually behave in this way but damn it I was horny as all fuck! My lazy ass husband was good for nothing and his cock hardly got up. But this dude had a rock-hard dick that I soon found myself riding hard and furious. I almost felt sorry for his huge balls as I smashed against them riding his steel shaft. I bounced every which way but loose all over his cock and his lap, and then I turned reverse cowgirl and fucked him nine ways to Sunday. My drenched velvet tunnel drenched his very horny love meat. As I reverse cowgirled his dick he grabbed my ass and helped me bounce even harder on his bronco.

It felt so fucking good riding the cum out of a strange dick. He then flipped me over on my back threw my legs over his shoulders and started to hammer my angry cunt. Fuck, he was screwing me hard and I loved every minute of it. It had been ages since I had been fucked so well. After we both had a screaming orgasm, I told him "Eat the fuck out of my gushing cunt and do it now!"

He did exactly as I asked. I spread my legs as far as they would go. I propped one foot on the nightstand and the other on the wall. The electrician dude went to town on my hairy snatch not missing a lick. He put about 220 volts through my clit with his cock...my cunt was like a high voltage outlet and he made my pussy's fuse blow.

He then pushed my head down on his lust wand and rammed it down my throat. It was long and reached back to my gag reflex. I nursed it for all it was fucking worth. It tasted like a horny and greedy dick as I swallowed the fuck out of it. I could taste the beginnings of pre-cum and I knew his rod was about to blow again. He groaned very loudly and spewed his big cock off straight down my greedy throat. It tasted like lust and sex combined in an intimate elixir.

The elixir tasted so fucking hot and it made my cunt squirt all over the bed at the same time. He and I both collapsed in heated exhaustion and then we broke out into laughter. I told him if I ever needed my box worked on again, I'd be sure to call him first. It's always a good idea to have a list of your local handymen around. Knowing how well they do at their job and how available they are can be a great thing to know. You never can tell when you might need an emergency visit, whether it's for an overheating appliance, or maybe your AC is broken and you are too hot and need help right away. I know my electrician inside and out and trust me he knows exactly how to fix my socket every time.

CHAPTER 3

UNCLOG MY PIPES

DAMN IT! Not again. It seems every time I try to flush my toilet it tries to run over these days. It seems to do so at least once a day now. I've had it, I'm calling a plumber to come and fix it ASAP. God, I hope they don't send over some beer-bellied guy that stinks and has his ass hanging out of his pants. Oh well! When a girl needs her pipes unclogged she needs them unclogged and that's all there is to it.

I thumbed through the yellow pages and came across an ad with the best looking of the worst looking in the ad picture. They were probably just models though, I thought as I dialed the number. I explained my plumbing problem and they said they'd send the dude out in a few hours. I figured that gave me time to sunbathe in the nude outside by my pool. I had a privacy fence so I really wasn't too worried about anyone seeing. I am an exhibitionist anyway. So even if old Mr. Klinkheimer next door sees my bald pussy getting tanned who cares! He probably needed the thrill.

I rubbed Hawaiian tropic all over my already tanned body and I laid there glistening like a shiny piece of aluminum foil. I drifted off to dreamland and failed to hear the plumber's truck pull up in my garage. Before I had time to think, I heard this, "Ma'am, are you back here? It's Joe with Pipes and Wrenches here to unclog your pipes." Oh my God! I sat up but not in time to cover myself before Joe swung open my gate and saw me lying there in my birthday suit.

"Oh I'm sorry ma'am!" exclaimed Joe running out the gate, but not before he gave my body a once over I noticed. By the way, Joe was hotter than fuck! I had never seen such a gorgeous fucking plumber in my whole life. He was tall, dark, and dreamy, and by the size of his hands, I figured his cock was long and hard as well. I swear I felt my cunt nearly explode. It definitely got drenched right there on the spot.

I slipped on my swimsuit cover colored a hot pink and flew inside to see what Joe was up to. I walked into the bathroom and I about fainted dead cold. Joe was standing there by my toilet wanking the fuck out of his long cock. It turned me on big time! Most ladies would probably be offended, but as I said, I am an exhibitionist and a nympho extraordinaire. "Holy fuck dude, you are hung like a horse!" I said before I could stop myself. The next thing I knew I dropped my bathing suit cover and dropped to my knees simultaneously.

Joe had his meat hanging out of his zipper. Apparently, my hot suntanned body turned him on so much he didn't even take the time to unbutton his pants. He simply unzipped and started jerking his dick. It was very apparent. Before either of us said a word, I had Joe's shaft in my hands sticking it down my greedy throat. I looked up at him with innocent little girl eyes while I choked and gagged on his long gun. His meat tasted so damn good. It tasted like a mixture of dick and the pussy he had screwed the night before, and I loved it. I am super kinky that way! Joe pushed my blonde head harder onto his nasty crotch and I could already taste the beginnings of his pre-cum drool. He then told me to bend my suntanned ass over and take his dangling snake in my burning cunt. "I'll unclog you real fucking fast," he said as he entered me with one thrust of his long and lean pipe. It felt fucking hot as he plunged me from behind with all the power he could muster.

He pushed me hard up against the water heater and roto-rooter the fuck out of my cream-clogged cunt. I squirmed and wiggled my tan-lined ass back up against his throbbing cunt pipe. He gave new meaning to the term ball cock. I'd ball his fucking cock time and time again. He was one of the best screws I had ever had, bar none.

He picked me up, held me up against his waist, and began fucking me and walking me towards the kitchen at the same time. Once we got there, he plopped me up on the countertop and started eating me out. His head wallowed back and forth on my clit and lips like a dog going after a steak bone. Damn, it felt so fucking awesome I almost fell off the fucking countertop. This dude knew his way around more than just pipes, that's for damn sure.

I pushed his greedy mouth harder into my craving cunt just begging him to eat the fuck out of it. Then before I knew what hit me I sprang my own leak and squirted all over his mouth and face. He shook his face off and my gush flew everywhere. I saw droplets of my pussy cum fly across the room as the sunlight coming in from the window turned them into sparkling droplets. I couldn't believe my eyes. Cum was flying everywhere.

.   .   .

The plumber, Joe, yanked out his nightstick and started jerking the fuck out of it and it popped off sending spew all over me, my face, my hair, and my already drenched pussy.

As I walked Joe out to his truck, I thanked him for a job well done. He told me if I ever needed any "plumbing" done to sure give him a call. I told him I would. Not only was my toilet flushing properly, but I was also no longer horny as hell. It seems to me that Joe knows his business when it comes to unclogging pipes and getting pussies off.

CHAPTER 4

COLOR ME PINK

I WAS FINALLY GETTING my bathroom repainted today and I was so excited I could hardly stand it. I had always wanted a pale pink bathroom decorated in the most feminine style. Today was the day I was going to get my wish. I had a painter coming over to paint my bathroom walls pink and I was well, tickled pink!

I got all of my toiletries and perfume and stuff out of the way so this guy could work without distractions. I had never met the dude. He just came highly recommended. About the time I got finished preparing my bathroom I hear a van pull up in my driveway. I sure hoped it was the painter, and by what I saw out my window, it was!

As he got closer to the door, I about fell out. He was a fucking hunk! I mean the type of Brad Pitt hunk you hardly ever see in day-to-day life. I walked over to him while he was mixing up my pink taffeta paint. I did my best to flirt with all of the female wiles I could muster. At first, he didn't seem to notice but then he looked up at my ample tits hanging from my very revealing hot pink top. I on purposely bent over so he could see them. I barely was able to contain them in my very low-cut tank top.

I could tell he liked what he saw and as I was bent over, I could see a decent-sized bulge in his white painter pants. It turned me on instantly. I had been single for a while and just itching to get laid. I knew I needed to stop thinking this way. I did not know this man. He was a complete stranger. I definitely needed to get the sexual thoughts off of my mind. I went inside the house and found myself daydreaming about the painter. I couldn't help it, so I came up with a daring yet brilliant idea. I draped a towel around me and headed for the bathroom. I noticed he was already starting to paint the back wall. I loved the color but I decided to do something brave. So I waltzed into the bathroom and said, "Mr. Painter, I like the pink but I want it more this shade" and then I dropped my towel revealing my pastel lips and pink nips.

He was so surprised and aroused he dropped his paint-brush. But he didn't bother to pick it up; he just latched onto my right pink nipple and started to suck gently but hungrily. It immediately got my pink pussy flaps quivering and my tunnel drenched. This guy was going to paint my throat a flushed hot pink if he didn't stop eating my tits so good. My lush pink nipples were points of delicious stiff-ness for this guy. He lapped them like he was licking a super-sweet lollipop. I suddenly had the desire to tickle his balls and his shaft pink with my expert mouth and luscious rose-colored lips. I slipped down to my knees and unzipped his white painter's pants and out popped his dick like a horse from a gate. His dick was hard as paint can and curved at the end. I popped the curved end of his redhead in and out of my cock hungry lips. The more I sucked the brighter and hotter pink it became.

He groaned and said, "I will bang you until your flower sprouts pink petals." I couldn't handle the temptation another second I got down on all four in doggie position and wiggled my hot ass high in the air as if to call him over to my starving velvet tunnel. He drag two wet fingers through my moistened rosy tunnel and I let out an animal growl. He popped my tight tush with a playful sting turning it a hot pink. I bounced my bum as if begging for his gun's entry. He put one finger inside my bum filling it fully and making my cookie even wetter than I thought she could get. My rear felt electrically charged and as if he had it plugged within the grasp of ecstasy.

While he worked my anus, I playfully tickled my clit and made it stand to rose-colored attention. His alabaster rod was now at the opening of my needy anus. With one long thrust, he plunged deep inside my tush. I could feel his skin sweating hot beads of liquid passion, slipping next to my flesh so slippery. He squeezed my buttocks with gropes of craving greed causing me to roar out like a she-wolf. His eyes were emblazoned with passionate yearning while the animal lust between us overtook the room with the scent of hot seduction filling every nuance within the atmosphere. Sensuality dripped from every pore on our molten bodies

We fucked for what seemed like hours but was truly only about 30 minutes. I helped the hot painter clean up the splattered pink paint so he could return back to work. I also thanked him for tickling me pink as well. He informed me that the pleasure was deliciously his and then my pink lips were the best he had ever sucked on. I informed him that his naughty cock was wild and fun and I thanked him for giving me the banging I had so desperately needed. He had performed more than one service here for damn sure. Once the time rolled around for this horny dude to leave, my bathroom was a cotton candy shade of pink. It was awesome and when I went to take a shower about 30 minutes later, my clit and lips were swollen to a pink that made me feel so horny. In fact, I felt so horny I jerked off in the shower and thought about the incredible banging I had just gotten. It was well worth my and my cunt's time to have the bathroom painted the color of my honey pussy.

CHAPTER 5

STONE COLD COCKED

I WAS SO EXCITED. I was getting new granite put down on my countertops today and I could not wait. I have always wanted elegant-looking granite in my kitchen. I may as well have it. I sure didn't have much else going for me in life. My husband was a cheating loser and I was one lonely MILF. My new granite was all I had to look forward to in life. I sure hadn't been laid in forever.

I couldn't wait for the tile man to get here to start setting my granite countertops. When he did get here and exited out of his van, I was shocked to see how hunky the guy was. I was going to have the double pleasure today. I was getting new granite countertops and getting to feast my eyes on a handsome dude. I watched his strong arms as he tediously brought the granite into my kitchen. I asked him, "Are you hot? Do you need to cool off?" He said, "A nice cool drink would go down good." So I went and got him a cold glass of iced tea. He thanked me and started to swallow with big gulps. I must admit I felt a twinge down south. I also felt my pointed nipples stand straight out on end. Fuck! What was happening? I was actually started to feel my pussy get slick and wet.

I tried to get my mind off of the front of his faded jeans but I could distinctly see the head of his cock lying to the side like a twitching snake underneath the pale fabric. I ran to the bathroom real quick and buried 3 fingers in my cunt. It felt like I was boiling inside...with a need for way more than three fingers. I pinched my nipples hard and bent down to suck on one. I tasted my cream from my third finger and then got so horny I knew I was about to fuck him. I could hardly stand it. The thought of his head pressed tight against his jeans made me ache to be screwed. So I reached for my trusty shampoo bottle filled with cool water and sat down on it for a few minutes. The cap felt like a hard cock head as I slid up and down on it each entrance grazed my g-spot and made me squirm with a need I felt my lips begin to grasp onto the side of the bottle with a suction sound.

That's it, I decided. I was going to go after that tile guy and become a complete nympho for the day. Why can't a girl have some fun every now and then? I slipped into my bedroom and threw on my see-through fishnet dress. This ought to get his attention I thought. Then I be-bopped my hot ass out to the kitchen area with my pointed nips poking through the fishnet as if they were peeking to see his cock themselves. The tile guy about got stuck in his mud when he took one look at my nude body underneath hot pink fishnet. He didn't need much of an imagination to enjoy my little show. It was all there out in the open for him to drool over, and his dick head too, I hoped. I swear I saw it move just a quarter-inch inside his faded, tight Levis. It seemed to strain hard against the zipper the more he feasted his eyes on me. His cock reminded me of why I was so glad to be a woman. I could almost feel it sliding into me as I saw it lying there growing beneath his jeans.

The more I looked at it the longer it seemed to grow. Talk about motivation to keep looking! I waited for him to make the first move. He waited for me. The minutes seemed like hours as we stood face to face wrapped up in the nuance of two bodies plagued by need. Our bodies were hungry and we were pulsating with red-hot ecstasy. We hungrily kissed as if our lives fucking depended on it.

His hands explored every inch of my throbbing body and he made it down to my cunt where he immediately plunged 2 fingers deep within it. I rode upon his finger as if I was sliding up and down on his rigid dick I could see bulging, just aching to pop out of the zipper it was contained in. I needed a good fuck, that's the truth. It had been a while. He told me to lean up against the counter on which he had been working and poke my pussy out. I did as he asked and he slowly but amazingly slipped inside my blushing peach one-half of an inch at a time if not one-quarter of an inch. It was excruciatingly delicious. I was like a child waiting on a chocolate dessert as he eased his shaft deep into my cock teaser.

This was one of those sexual experiences that you knew you shouldn't have but it felt so fucking good you didn't care. The reason it felt so hot was that it was forbidden. I rolled over onto my back while the tile guy explored every inch of my pussy with his hungry mouth. It felt amazing as I felt my cum getting ready to release into his mouth. I couldn't hold back any longer and I came all over his face while drops of my white cream dripped onto the black granite. I returned the oral pleasure to him and went down balls deep onto his throbbing and swollen cock. He groaned like a roaring tiger and exploded deep into my throat nearly gagging me with his heavy load.

That was a day I will never forget. Not only did I get the most beautiful granite countertops installed, but I also had one of the most erotic sexual rendezvous of my life. Now that I think about it, I may just decide to have my kitchen floors tiled. It sounded like an exciting idea to me in more ways than one if you catch my drift.High Voltage

He was climbing on the ladder. Mary tried hard not to stare at him but couldn't help herself. He was breathtaking. Blonde, tall, and his muscles showed off under his tight gray shirt with every move. She could tell he had a six-pack. A quiet sigh escaped her, but it was loud enough for the maintenance guy to notice.

He smirked, his piercing blue eyes focusing on her. Mary's cheeks burned as she blushed.

Embarrassed she lowered her eyes to examine the floor closely.

"Are you okay?" His soft deep voice filled the room and made her heart beat faster. It was almost impossible to ignore the grin that lay in his words.

"Yes... yes, thank you," she stuttered, her face turning fiery red.

With a twinkle in his eyes, he smiled at her, making her turn away to leave so she could hide her blushed cheeks. But she didn't think about the wall that was right behind her. She heard his amused laughter as she realized her mistake.

This was going great, she thought. He must have thought she was stupid. "You sure you are okay?" he asked, still laughing.

Mary turned to face him and nodded.

"Funny," he winked. "I didn't know I had that kind of effect on women." A bolt of lightning struck Mary. Or at least it felt like it.

"No... I mean... I just..." She tried to find words to explain the situation and her odd behavior.

Well, of course, she acted as if she was dumb, and of course, it was because of him. After all, he was the personification of her hottest dreams. She didn't think when she called the company to have an electrician sent to her aid that it would turn out to be Mr. Perfect.

"It's alright." His smile was warm and friendly. "I think you're hot, too."

Mary was stupefied. Did he just say what she thought he said? With big brown eyes, she stared at him, unable to speak or move.

Step by step, he climbed down the ladder to stand right in front of her, looking deeply into her
eyes.

"You're really sexy and I'd like to do more with you than just talk about the lamp." His face got so close to hers she could feel his breath on her skin.

"I want you," he whispered, right before his lips touched hers.

His kiss was amazing. She forgot about everything around her, she just felt the intensity of this

kiss. And there she knew she wanted more, too.

With determination, her hand felt for the zipper of his pants, making him smile and unbutton her blouse. A sigh escaped her as he began to massage her full breasts. But she could tell he enjoyed it as much as she did since the bump in his jeans just got bigger.

In order to free his arousal, she finally unzipped his pants and without thinking about her actions went down on her knees. She wanted to feel him, taste him, make him moan.

He took a sharp and deep breath when her lips parted for his stone-hard erection, to let it slowly glide into her mouth. Her tongue started to carefully caress his most sensitive part, making him close his eyes in pleasure. He placed his hand on the back of her head and began to guide her moves. He wanted it hard and fast, Mary could tell. He pushed her head firmly towards himself while his hardness was sliding in and out of her mouth. His breath became heavier and was interrupted with quiet groans.

"You're so good at this," he panted. "Don't stop."

Mary loved how she was able to make this irresistible, strong guy so weak, to make him ask for more. Right now she was able to control him; if she wanted, she could stop and leave him like this. Or she could make him come. In her mouth.

"Mmh," she sighed inevitably, sucking him harder and letting her hand glide under her skirt, right between her legs. While pleasing him, she couldn't refuse herself some pleasure. Her hips started moving back and forth, in the same rhythm his erection was going in and out of her mouth.

"Oh man," he gasped. "You're going to make me come soon."

As a response, she took his hardness deep in her mouth and intensely played with it using her tongue, not stopping rubbing herself.

"Oh fuck," he yelled and pushed her head as close to him as possible. "Come on, suck it harder."

Sighing and moaning, Mary obeyed. His words turned her on so much. "Yeah, like this." He was hardly able to speak anymore.

With a few more pushes in her mouth, he finally couldn't hold it any longer. He held her head close and released all his sexual tension into it, groaning loudly.

"Don't think that this was it," he mumbled ecstatically while Mary still had his member between her lips. "I've got a lot more for you."

CHAPTER 6

THE SEXY PLUMBER

MY INSTINCTS WERE RIGHT; she was not wearing any panties. When she came to the door, seductively swinging her hips from left to right and giving me little grins as she led me to her kitchen, the one thought that had crossed my mind was that I hoped she was not wearing any panties with that mini skirt.

I stood less than an inch behind her, lusting at her gorgeous petite body. Her husband was not at home as usual and coincidentally her pipes were broken just when he had left for work. This was a convenient excuse to call her favorite handsome young stud. This was not the first time she was calling me in to work on her pipes when her husband was not around. However, in the past, she would be dressed in a plain pair of jeans and a t-shirt; nothing too revealing. Today was different; Ma-Ling was up to *no* good. She had every intention of seducing me and I loved her tease. The excessive flirting, the little smiles, the revealing clothing, and the biggest hint of all was the fact that she wore no panties. The way her nipples seemed to pierce through the fabric of her blouse also led me to believe that she was also without a bra.

"Let me have a closer look. Can you bend over and show me again?" I asked one last time.

She gave me an intense stare. She had a dangerous look in her eyes; the look of hunger and desire. Ma-Ling bent over slowly, popping her ass out and pretending to look under her kitchen sink.

"Ah, yes, I think I see it," I said pushing my groin against her ass. My hands soon began probing her slender legs, caressing her smooth bare skin. Working my way upwards, I found her already moist pussy. "I see you have something else that's dripping wet," I teased, stroking her wetness.

"Yes, Mr. Tony, long time..." she cooed in her heavy Chinese accent. "Really? *Long-time*..." I mocked pulling her in even closer.

She let out a little moan as she slowly began grinding her bum against my groin.

"Ma-Ling," I whispered as I continued to stroke the moist flesh of her invitingly warm pussy.

My dick throbbed in anticipation as she let out a little moan of pleasure. I needed to feel her tender flesh hugging my raw meat. The thought of her petite body going wild as I penetrated her temple of delight with my massive shaft was astounding.

"I want to hear you say it Ma-Ling. Say you want that big cock in your pussy," I ordered, yanking her long, silky jet-black hair and forcing her to stand to her feet. My lean body easily towered over hers.

"Yes Mr. Tony, I want it," she begged in a sexy voice.

"You want what," I yanked her by her hair even harder, pulling her body against mine. "Your dick!" she shrieked in pain.

That was all I needed to hear. The sound of her squeaky little voice begging for my dick was enough motivation for me to fuck her right there in her kitchen.

I captured her soft lips with my hungry mouth, giving her a hot passionate kiss. The urgency and desire that I felt for her were transferred from my body to hers and she instantly began kissing me back with just as much passion.

As we kissed, I took a few steps forward, pinning her body against the stainless steel refrigerator while ripping off her clothing. Once naked, I pulled back a little to take a good look at her gorgeous body. She was so slender, yet very attractive in her own right. Her perky little breasts seemed to call my name, *"Tony, Tony, Tony."*

She purred, whispering something in Chinese, just as I captured her hardened nipple with my mouth. My tongue moved feverishly over and around her nipple, sucking it occasionally. I used my hand to fondle her other breast, gently pulling and pinching the nipple. Ma-Ling seemed to thoroughly enjoy it when I gently bit her nipple, so much so that she asked me to do it even harder.

I let out a soft groan as her fingers stroked my body. She was caressing my muscular arms while moaning out in delirium. Our desire for each other grew and soon I was unbuckling my tool belt and loosening up my pants.

There was a loud rattling noise as the tool belt hit the floor. She opened her eyes, which had been closed, and looked down at it. She then brought her gaze back up, pulling my lips away from her nipple. I gave her a questionable look. Did she change her mind about this? No, she hadn't. She smiled, capturing my lips with hers for a brief moment, before eventually dropping down to her knees.

"Ma-Ling," was all I managed to say, as she whipped out my semi-erect cock and took it into her lust-filled mouth.

She was sucking my dick slowly, with her tongue flicking a few times over its head, causing it to gradually become harder and harder. She increased her suction on my manhood, giving me a series of longer harder sucks and making slurping noises every time she finished sucking the full length. I cocked my head back, letting out a loud groan. Tiny spasms were shooting through my body as she worked her tongue all over my dick. The more she sucked, the greater my desire to fuck her became. I'd soon had enough and could not take one more minute of her torture.

"Stand up," I ordered in a husky voice.

She pulled her lips from my dick and looked up. There was a little hesitation from her as if she didn't want to stop. She must have really been enjoying *Big T,* I thought. Big T was the name that I had given to my dick.

I didn't like the fact that she was becoming so comfortable that she was now beginning to be disobedient. I loved a sexy, submissive woman.

"Stand up!" I ordered in a firm voice, letting her know that I was becoming very impatient with her delay. As if she could have read my mind, she immediately sprung to her feet and apologized.

"Good penis, Mr. Tony. I like it a lot," she cooed, giving me a sheepish smile. *Penis? Who said that word anymore?* I thought to myself. Obviously, this woman was in way over her head. She had just tried to seduce the wrong guy. I was not a penis type of man; I was a cock type of man. I was a strong dominating man who enjoyed a woman that could satisfy my sexual appetite.

"Oh Ma-Ling, I'm going to destroy that pussy," I whispered in her ear, biting the earlobe lightly.

She moaned out, telling me "yes, yes," oblivious to the fact that I wanted nothing more than to see her wail in pain as my enormously large cock rammed in and out of her tight little pussy.

I finally decided to give Mrs. Ma-Ling Chen exactly what she'd called me over here for.

Bracing her body against the wall, I penetrated her pussy from the back. She moaned out loud as I fisted her hair while launching my body against hers viciously.

"Ahhh...Yes..." she moaned as I slammed my dick into her fun box. The side of her face pressed against the wall as I increased the force and momentum of my thrusting. Her deliciously warm pussy was so tight, tighter than I had imagined. It hugged my dick perfectly as its sweet juices trickled down my raw meat. I could literally feel the tiny contractions of her pussy on my dick. That let me know that she was having just as much fun as I was. Over and over I penetrated her wetness while she moaned out in ecstasy.

"Stop coming on my dick, Ma-Ling," I warned in a stern, husky voice. "Ah..." she moaned, ignoring my warning.

"Okay you don't wanna," I scolded, wrapping my arm around her neck and pulling her body against my dick harder than before. I now had her in the exact position that I wanted. Without further hesitation, I began serving her with a series of hard powerful thrusts that sent her body jerking forward viciously.

Ma-Ling moaned out, her voice cracking under the pressure of my penetrations. I felt a little sorry for her, she was so petite, and her pussy was so tight. My huge dick would destroy her little pussy, and so I eased off a little, giving her some slow long thrusts. After all, I did not want to hurt the poor woman; I just wanted to have a little fun with her. Her cries, previously of pain, changed to moans of pleasure and ecstasy.

"Oh...Oh...Mr...Ton..." she moaned, bucking her pussy against my dick as I increased the momentum of my thrusts. I was now slamming my dick into her juicy wet pussy, relentless, forgetting about everything else at the time. In and out my dick went, stretching her pussy beyond its limits.

Her kitchen was filled with our moaning and crying as the intensity of the moment drove us closer and closer to our earth-shattering climax.

"Ahhh...Shit...I'm coming..." I let out a long prolonged groan, gripping the top of her hip and thrusting my dick deeper and harder inside her. I exploded a load of my hot cum into her temple of delight while she too let out loud screams of pleasure as her juices coated my dick. We both had summited our amazing climax. Her pussy quivered on my dick as I took in deep breaths, trying to calm down from our moment of delirium.

It took us a moment to get our clothes together and get dressed. Turns out she did have a small leak in one of the pipes in the kitchen and it took me a few minutes to make the repair.

Before long, I was getting ready to leave her home.

"Thank you so much. I don't know what I would do without you," she smiled as she handed me the check for $100, which was my service fee. She slipped me an additional $50 with a little grin. I wanted to refuse her little tip, but she insisted, saying that it was for everything else that I'd done. I almost felt like a cheap little man-whore, but I reminded myself that I'd just gotten some really good pussy. Besides, she didn't even have to give me any more than my fee, but she'd been generous enough to give me a little bonus. What the hell! If she was going to pay me to fuck the hell out of her, then that was just icing on the cake.

ABOUT THE AUTHOR

Melisa Poche is an emerging erotica author of many erotica kinks and sub-genres. Be sure to check out other books and leave a review if this story got you hot!

Visit my blog at Melisa Poche Blog

Join my newsletter for exclusive Melisa Poche Newsletter

Sign up for Free Stories from Xplicit Press Authors

Xplicit Press Author UpdatesShon Gacy Newsletter

Like Xplicit Press on Facebook

Follow Xplicit Press on Twitter

Readers: I want to expand a few of the stories to see where the characters can be explored further. If there are any of the stories that you would like to read more about again, I'd love to hear from you!

Keep In Touch
Melisa Poche
info@melisapoche.com